Peanut Butter and Jelly

#4

TROUBLE AT ALCOTT SCHOOL

**Look for these and other books
in the PEANUT BUTTER
AND JELLY series:**

#4

TROUBLE AT ALCOTT SCHOOL

Dorothy Haas

Illustrated by Jeffrey Lindbergh

A
LITTLE APPLE
PAPERBACK

SCHOLASTIC INC.
New York Toronto London Auckland Sydney

ISBN 0-590-41509-3

12 11 10 9 8 7 6 5 4 3 2 1   9/8 0 1 2 3 4/9

Printed in the U.S.A.   11

First Scholastic printing, August 1989

*Remembering my
dear friend
Mary Ann*

CHAPTER
1

"It's old," said Erin. "I mean really old. My great-aunt Dody got it from her mother when she was ten." She slid a finger under the yellow ribbon that held the gold locket and lifted it away from her sweater so that Peanut and Jilly could admire it.

Polly Butterman, known to her friends as Peanut, touched the red stone on the locket. "A real ruby," she said in wonder.

Erin shook her head. "It's a garnet. My mom said that lots of antique jewelry had garnets."

Jillian Matthews fingered the little gold pancake. "Is there something in it?"

Erin, her chin dug into her chest so she could see what she was doing, pried open the locket. Inside was a fuzzy picture of a young girl, her hair done up in an old-fashioned way, looking shyly at the camera.

"It's Great-aunt Dody," said Erin, "when she was a girl. Wasn't she pretty?"

"We've got some funny old pictures in our album," said Peanut. "My mom's grandmother dressed in the weirdest way. I mean, she played tennis wearing a long skirt!"

"I'm going to get my grandmother's gold bracelet someday," said Emmy. "I can't have it till I'm older, though. You're lucky to have the locket now, Erin."

Peanut and Jilly, coming out of the girls' lavatory, had bumped into Erin and Emmy. They had all stopped right there in the doorway to admire Erin's locket. It was, they agreed, the most romantic thing any of them owned.

"I'm not supposed to wear it every day, though," said Erin. "It's just for Sunday and

3

parties. Between times, my mother only lets me take it out and look at it."

Jilly remembered something. "When I was little, I used to take everything out of my mother's jewelry box and try on all the earrings and necklaces. I hated putting them away. Especially the earrings."

"Will you *please* not *block* the door." The long-suffering voice came from behind them. "Other people have the right to use this girls' room, too, you know."

Peanut and Jilly rolled their eyes and stepped aside.

Jennifer Patimkin started to pass them. The worst thing about Jennifer was that she was a pain in the neck. She didn't even have to work at it — being a pain in the neck seemed to come naturally to her. The best thing about her was that she was in Mr. Moore's class, not Miss Kraft's. That meant Peanut and Jilly didn't have to put up with her all day long.

Jennifer paused, staring at Erin's locket.

"It's really, really old," said Peanut. "Erin's great-aunt gave it to her."

Jennifer leaned close to look at the locket. She smiled sweetly. "It's pretty in a sort of old-fashioned way, I guess. Of course, I'd much rather have something up to date. I've never cared for second-hand things."

She swept on into the lavatory.

Erin's cheeks flushed. Her eyes crinkled. She looked as though she might cry.

"That Jennifer," sputtered Peanut. "She gets more hateful by the day. She thinks it's fun to make people feel terrible."

Jilly hugged Erin. "She's just green with envy."

"She's jealous because she doesn't have a locket with a garnet in it," said Emmy.

The bell rang and they moved toward their classroom, crowding around Erin to help her feel better. Inside, they went to their desks.

Peanut settled into her seat and took out her science book. She opened it to the place where they had left off yesterday and looked toward the front of the room.

A slender woman was writing on the chalkboard, her back to the class. Who was she?

Her hair was brown and caught up in a loose knot on top of her head. She was wearing a high-necked blouse with lace around the cuffs. Her skirt went right down to the floor. Where was Miss Kraft?

The room had grown still, all eyes fixed on the stranger. Peanut and Jilly locked eyes across the room. What was going on? Was Miss Kraft sick? Substitute teachers weren't much fun. Nobody was as much fun as Miss Kraft. And what was the woman drawing?

Clue was written on the board. Beside it was a picture of the inside of a leg, the bones showing — an X ray.

"Good morning, scholars. I present you with a conundrum this morning. Who am I? What did I do? When did I do it?"

The woman turned. It *was* Miss Kraft! But what a changed Miss Kraft! Her hair was hidden under a wig — for surely the brown hair was a wig. With her floor-dusting skirt and her frilly blouse with a cameo pinned at the throat, she looked as though she had stepped out of another century. Miss Kraft was doing another of her projects.

The room rustled as everyone settled back, relieved that Miss Kraft wasn't taking the day off.

"What's a con — con — that drum thing you said?" asked Elvis.

"Co-nun-drum." Miss Kraft said the word slowly. "A puzzle. Something to guess." She did and she did not sound like Miss Kraft. She sounded as though she did not speak English well.

"Can we ask you questions?" asked Ollie.

"*May* you ask me questions," said Miss Kraft. "Yes, you may."

"Why are you wearing that funny-looking hair?" asked Ollie. "It looks like a bird's nest."

Everybody groaned. Trust Ollie to say something awful.

"Ladies of my day wear their hair long," said Miss Kraft. "I pin it up on top of my head."

"Safety pins in your head?" asked Elvis, giggling.

"Young man," said Miss Kraft, "I would ask

7

you to be serious. *Pins* means *hairpins.* All the ladies of my day use hairpins to hold their hair in place."

Peanut had been looking down at her science book. "You had something to do with science, I bet."

Miss Kraft nodded. *"Très bien,"* she said.

"You're French," Jilly said excitedly. *"Très bien* means very good in French. So you must be French."

"Welllll." Miss Kraft drew out the word. "Yes and no."

"Did you invent something?" asked David.

Miss Kraft shook her head. No.

"Discovered, then?" said Peanut. "Did you discover something?"

"Partly," said Miss Kraft. "Yes, I partly discovered something."

Jilly zeroed in on the picture on the board. One of the bones was broken. "You can't see the bones in a leg unless you go to the hospital and have it X-rayed," she said.

"Vraiment," said Miss Kraft. "True."

"So, did you discover X rays?" asked David.

"What makes X rays?" asked Miss Kraft.

"Radium," said Peanut. "Did you discover radium?"

"*Oui.* Yes. But I did not do this great discovery alone," said Miss Kraft. "My husband and I, we did this together. Who am I?"

"Give us another clue," begged Emmy.

"What are X rays used for?" asked Miss Kraft.

"To make you well."

"To show what's wrong with you."

"So you can be healed of what's wrong."

The answers came from around the room.

"Do you know another word that means heal?" asked Miss Kraft.

"Cure?" said Peanut, who was pretty good about remembering words.

"You are close to my name," said Miss Kraft. "Very close."

"Curie?" asked David. "There was a woman named Curie. She was a big scientist."

"*Très bien,*" said Miss Kraft. "I am Marie Curie. My husband and I — "

"*Yike!*"

9

The shriek came from Courtney. Everyone turned to see what was going on.

"Elvis's mice are loose," she gasped. "I don't like mice, even the white ones."

"Elvis, what in the world?" Miss Kraft called above the bedlam, forgetting her accent.

"They jumped out of my pocket," said Elvis. "Quick! We've got to catch 'em." He dived toward the corner, where one of the mice was disappearing into the supply cabinet.

Everyone jumped. They scurried around the room after the other mouse.

At the front of the room, Miss Kraft covered her eyes with her hand. "Nothing in this class goes the way I plan it." She sighed. "Nothing."

CHAPTER 2

"Got 'em!" Elvis said a few minutes later. "Both of 'em."

"Two mice?" asked Miss Kraft. "And you brought them to school in your pocket? That's hardly the best carrying method for mice."

"They like my pocket. I guess because it's warm," said Elvis. "I thought we could see how they act and everything. I mean, since we're doing science stuff this month."

"I thought your mother said you couldn't keep your mice anymore, Elvis," said Kevin.

"Well, see, I'm not keeping them," said Elvis.

11

"I mean, they aren't at home if they're here."

"I see," said Miss Kraft, looking as though she understood a lot more than she was saying. "You can't keep your mice at home. That's really why you brought them to school."

Elvis grinned. "We can learn a whole lot from these mice."

Miss Kraft sighed. "All right, Elvis. We can keep them here and study them. But just for a few days. I think we have a cage left over from our gerbil project. That might work for the mice. David, you will find it at the back of the storage closet. Food and a water bottle are right there with it. Elvis, what do we need to make the mice comfortable?"

"Just food," said Elvis. "And water."

Emmy and Erin went to fill the water bottle.

Jilly dug out some newspapers to line the cage.

Peanut looked at the M volume of the encyclopedia to see if the mice needed anything else. "They need a kind of little house," she said. "Maybe we can cut a door and windows in a Kleenex box."

Soon the mice were settled in their new home on the top shelf of the bookcase under the windows.

"I brought some corn for them," said Elvis, taking a plastic bag out of his pocket and pouring dried kernels into the food cup.

"They can have some of my apple," said Jilly, offering it to the mice through the wire. One of them nibbled at it. "They're really tame," she said. "This one's eating from my fingers."

"Have they got names?" Ollie asked. "Or do you just call them Mouse One and Mouse Two?"

"I call them Roll and Rock," said Elvis. "Get it? Rock and Roll?"

Everyone groaned.

"But we can give them new names," Elvis went on. "The neat thing about mice is, they don't care if you change their names."

Peanut remembered what they had been

doing when the mice got loose. Miss Kraft was still standing at the front of the room in her brown wig and long skirt, her new project forgotten.

"Why don't we call them Marie and Curie?" Peanut suggested.

"Hey, how about Raidy and Yum?" said Elvis. "Get it? Raidy-Yum?"

"Corny," muttered Ollie.

"Whose mice are they, anyway?" asked Elvis.

Miss Kraft clapped her hands. "All right, people. Let's get back to what we were doing before we were interrupted by Raidy" — she looked pained — "and Yum."

"You said yes and no about being French," said Jilly. "Why?"

"My name is Marie Sklodowska Curie," said Miss Kraft. "What does a name like Sklodowska sound like?"

"Polish," said Nate. "My grandma came from Poland. Are you Polish?"

Miss Kraft nodded. She sounded foreign

14

again. "I am an expatriate." She said the word slowly. Ex-pay-tree-ate. "That means I live outside my native land. I study and work in France. I am married to Pierre Curie. We received the Nobel prize for our work on radioactivity and radium."

Peanut listened avidly. It was wonderful to learn about people by having them visit the class, as Miss-Kraft-Marie-Curie was doing. It was a little like being right in a TV play.

"Now," said Miss Kraft, "I want all of you to think about people you might become. I want you to read about different scientists and be prepared to tell us about yourselves."

Jilly turned and met Peanut's eyes. Who would she be? What famous scientist?

"Let's go to the Learning Center together." Peanut mouthed the words silently.

Jilly caught what she was saying and nodded. It would be fun to read up on the scientists together and —

"Ohhhhhh!" Erin's wail lifted over Miss Kraft's voice. "My locket. It's gone! It's gone."

15

Again Miss Kraft was forgotten as everyone stood up and looked at Erin. Peanut and Jilly and Emmy went to her.

"Oh, Erin," said Jilly, "it's got to be right here."

"Is it on the floor?" asked Emmy.

"Did it slide inside your sweater?" asked Peanut.

Erin touched her neck . . . patted the front of her sweater . . . reached inside her sweater and felt around her middle. She shook her head.

Looking sad and scared, her eyes big, she searched her desk and crawled around on the floor underneath her desk.

"It's not here," she said in a small voice.

"But it's got to be," said Peanut. "You had it on just before class began."

"Maybe it's in Raidy and Yum's cage," said Elvis, going to look. "Don't worry," he said over his shoulder. "I don't think mice like to eat stuff like lockets. Nope, it's not here," he called from the other side of the room.

"Maybe she dropped it when we went to fill

16

the water bottle," said Emmy. She lifted her eyes to Miss Kraft for permission to leave the room.

"You may go," said Miss Kraft.

Emmy and Erin ran for the door.

"Walk," Miss Kraft called. "Don't run in the hall."

They didn't hear her. They were already through the door and running toward the drinking fountain.

"While we're waiting, I'd really like us to move ahead with our science studies," said Miss Kraft.

They all returned to their seats.

Peanut didn't hear what Miss Kraft was saying. How terrible to lose a beautiful, antique locket, one with a real garnet in it. What would Erin tell her great-aunt when she asked where the locket was next time she came to visit? Peanut shuddered.

Everyone turned when Emmy and Erin came back into the room.

"It isn't anywhere," said Emmy. "We looked everywhere."

Erin's eyes were full of tears. "What'll I tell my mother?" she said, her voice quivering. "I wasn't supposed to wear the locket to school. My mother didn't know I brought it with me."

Miss Kraft went to her and slipped an arm around her shoulders. "The locket has to be here someplace. I'm certain we'll find it."

"Maybe it fell off and stuck to the bottom of somebody's shoes," said Ollie. "It would've done that, if someone has gum on their shoes."

There was a stir as everyone checked their shoes. But the shoes were gum — and locket — free.

"We'll take ten minutes and give the room one last good search," said Miss Kraft. "Then we'll have to get on with our work."

They scoured the room, looking in all the corners, under the desks, around the book-shelves, in the storage closet. But the locket seemed to have disappeared into the air.

"Maybe," said Courtney when they settled back into their seats, "somebody here took it."

"Well, *I* sure didn't."

"What would I want with a dumb girl's locket?"

"I didn't rip it off. Ripping off — that's the same as stealing."

The voices lifted, arguing, defensive.

"All right now!" Miss Kraft spoke sharply. "That's a serious thing to say, Courtney. Can you see how it makes everyone feel?"

"I'm sorry," Courtney muttered. "Only it's so funny to have Erin's locket gone and we're all right here."

"We must not be suspicious of each other," said Miss Kraft. "We are good friends, a good working group. We must not be split up by suspicion."

There was a general muttering.

"Let's get on with our work. Your locket will turn up in some unlikely place, Erin. We don't know where or when. But it's here someplace."

Erin didn't look sure of that. But they all settled down to work.

"You don't really suppose maybe someone did take it, do you?" asked Peanut later on

20

when she and Jilly went to the Learning Center to look up famous scientists.

Jilly bit her lip, looking worried. "Once you get an idea like that, it's hard not to think about it. It's like not thinking about a purple hippopotamus once somebody says 'purple hippopotamus.'"

"But you can laugh about a purple hippo," said Peanut. "You can't laugh if you think someone we know took Erin's locket."

Troubled, they started looking through the science biographies.

CHAPTER
3

"What did your mother say when you told her about the locket?" Peanut asked the next morning as they were stowing their coats in their lockers.

Erin looked glum. "She didn't scold. She said losing it was enough punishment. She said I'm always going to remember the locket and wish I hadn't worn it to school when I wasn't supposed to."

"What about your great-aunt?" asked Jilly. "What are you going to tell her?"

Erin shuddered. "She lives in Milwaukee, so she doesn't come to visit us a lot. I hope she never comes to see us again. Then I'll never have to tell her."

"But you can't wish not to see her!" Peanut protested. "She's your favorite aunt."

"If you never see her again," said Jilly, "it means you've lost both your locket *and* your aunt."

It was all so terrible they could only stare at each other.

In the days that followed, they learned a lot about taking care of white mice, a lot about Madame Curie, and a lot about other scientists. But they didn't find the locket.

Elvis liked taking the mice out of their cage and letting them walk around on his shoulders. One morning he even put a kernel of corn in his right ear and let one of the mice pick it up.

"Ick," said Courtney. "How can you stand them walking around on you like that?" She made a face. "I'd never wear that shirt again."

Elvis laughed. "They're clean," he said, "and

soft. You ought to hold them. You'd see. Here —
take Yum."

Courtney backed away, her hands behind
her back. "I'd rather die."

In addition to reading about scientists and
deciding which ones they would like to be,
Peanut and Jilly did a project together about
Poland and what it was like when Marie Curie
lived there.

"Her name was Marie Sklodowska," Jilly
told the class the day they did their report.
"Polish women have different endings on their
names than men do. Like, her father was
called Sklodowski."

"Russia took over Warsaw," said Peanut.
"The people didn't have their freedom. But
they treasured the Polish ways of doing things."

"Frédéric Chopin was a Polish composer,"
said Jilly. "He lived in France, too. He wrote
music about Poland called polonaises."

"Marie Curie discovered a new metal," said
Peanut. "She called it polonium."

"She was the first person to win two Nobel
prizes," said Jilly.

"I'd feel terrible if I had to leave my country and live someplace else," said Peanut. "I'd miss the Fourth of July and eating at McDonald's."

"I'd miss Thanksgiving and singing 'The Star-Spangled Banner'," said Jilly.

"Well done, girls," said Miss Kraft. "You've given the class some understanding of what Madame Curie's feelings for her country must have been. Now, David, suppose you tell us about radium."

While David talked, Peanut closed her notebook and glanced across the rows at Jilly. They grinned at each other, pleased with what they had done. They had tossed the subject back and forth between them as though they were playing ball. It was fun working together. What one of them forgot, the other remembered.

To think that she and Jilly had hated each other when she moved here from Minneapolis! How funny! It was only in working together, in researching each other, that they had become best friends.

"We're a team," Peanut thought. "A team of two."

She still thought about Regan sometimes, though. . . .

It was when they were on their way to the lunchroom — pretending not to see Jennifer and her friends when they passed them in the hall — that something happened. Erin stopped at her locker to get her lunch. Almost everyone ate whatever Mrs. Donovan cooked at noon. But Erin didn't. Erin always brought her own sandwich from home. She ate the same sandwich every day — sliced egg, ketchup, and pickle relish.

"I know for sure what's in my sandwich," she said. "I know I'm going to like it. But I might not like what Mrs. Donovan fixes for lunch."

While Erin poked around in her locker, Peanut and Jilly and Emmy waited. Emmy told them how she was dying to have her ears pierced, but her mother had said she would have to wait until she was twelve. And she wouldn't change her mind no matter how much Emmy begged.

Suddenly Peanut looked past Emmy. Erin was standing at the open door of her locker, staring down at a piece of paper.

"Erin?" asked Peanut. "What's wrong?"

Erin looked up. Her mouth opened and closed like a guppy's. Without saying a word, she held out the paper. Something was printed on it in green marker.

Peanut and Jilly and Emmy crowded close to read it.

Lucy Pocket lost her locket,
Kitty Fisher found it.
There was not a penny in it.
But a ribbon on it.
Stay tuned for more news.

"Someone's found my locket," Erin breathed. "But why don't they just give it to me? I mean, why write a goofy note about it?"

"That's a Mother Goose rhyme," said Peanut. "Only it's turned around. It was Lucy Locket.

28

And she lost her pocket. That's a purse."

"How did the note get into your locker?" asked Jilly.

"I guess they just slid it in through the crack at the bottom," said Erin.

"Who would send you a note?" asked Emmy.

"Two notes," said Peanut. "It says stay tuned. So that means whoever has it is going to send another note."

Erin picked up her lunch and they went on their way to the lunchroom.

Peanut was angry. "Whoever wrote that note is really mean. They're just sitting out there — whoever they are — watching Erin squirm."

Jilly was thoughtful. "Honestly I don't think anyone we know would be so mean. Nobody in our room would do that."

As they got into line to pick up their milk, Erin smiled. It was the first time she had smiled since she lost the locket. "I'm going to get my locket back," she said. "I just know I am. I'll be so glad. And I'll never have to tell my aunt I lost it."

CHAPTER
4

Peanut and Jilly were alone. Both of Peanut's sisters were out. Maggie was at volleyball practice. Ceci was at a meeting of the debate club. Only Nibbsie was there to give Peanut a big welcome. She gathered him up. "Glad to see me, Nibs? Hmmm?"

She got a quick lick on the nose in reply.

"Everyone's gone and you feel lonesome, don't you, Nibbs?" she said. "Well, we're here now. We're your true friends. Right?"

Nibbsie's tail swished. He was so happy to

see her that Peanut felt like the nicest person in town.

She turned to Jilly and dumped Nibbsie into her arms. "Say hello. He needs lots of big hugs when he's been alone."

Jilly liked the feel of the fluffy little dog wriggling in her arms. She rubbed her chin on the top of his head. "He likes me more than he used to. Remember how he didn't used to want me to hold him?"

"He knows you're my friend," said Peanut.

A note was propped up on the telephone table at the foot of the stairs. "My mom's gone to the dentist and shopping," Peanut said, reading it. "She says maybe she'll be home when we get here, but maybe she won't. Well, I guess she's not. Let's get something to eat."

She went through the living room, turning on lamps as she passed them, heading toward the kitchen. "It feels funny to come home when the house is empty."

Jilly followed her. She thought for a minute. "I don't think I ever came home when nobody was there. My dad's always up in his studio."

Peanut turned on the dining room light and went into the kitchen, turning on that light, too. "I don't like it when nobody's here." She flicked on the radio and music filled the room.

She put popcorn in the microwave and found soda in the refrigerator.

"Cream soda?"

"Uh-uh. Grape."

"Cherry's good with popcorn. There's some of that diet kind in here, too," Peanut said over her shoulder. "Ceci drinks that. She's scared of getting fat. But my mom says she doesn't want me to drink it. She says I still need energy."

They sipped their soda, waiting for the popcorn to be finished.

"You know, it's really weird, that note Erin got," said Peanut. "It sounds like someone's trying to be funny. Only they aren't funny at all."

"It's not a *joke* kind of joke," said Jilly. "It's a ha-ha-I'm-teasing-you kind of joke. I hate to be teased. Jerry does that to me a lot. I really hate my brother sometimes."

"It's like when I was a little kid," said Peanut, "there was this girl who'd walk past me and say 'Ha-ha — I know something you don't know.' "

The microwave beeped. The popcorn was ready. Peanut poured it into a bowl, got some puppy biscuits for Nibbsie, and led the way upstairs to her room. They stretched out on the braided rug beside the bunk beds, the bowl of popcorn between them.

Peanut offered a biscuit to Nibbsie. He sat up and yipped and took it from her fingers. "Who wrote that note?" she asked. "Who would do that?"

"Ollie?" Jilly said it as though she didn't believe it.

"Uh-uh. He's not mean. Anyway, he'd have given himself away by calling Erin Lockethead or something. Who else? Not Elena!"

"Never! She wouldn't take something that doesn't belong to her. Did you know she goes to church with her mother every morning before school?"

"David wouldn't, either. He's so kind to

everybody. Have you ever noticed how he sticks up for Kevin whenever someone calls him dumb?"

"And Courtney wouldn't. She'd make up a brand-new poem, not copy one out of Mother Goose."

"Allison wouldn't. She hugged Erin when Erin was feeling so bad. And anyway, she's got a locket. It hasn't got a garnet in it, though."

They made a list of their classmates and then, one by one, considered each of them. Nate . . . Kevin . . . Carrie . . . Rachel . . . Beth . . . Todd . . . Luke. . . . They reached the end of the list and Jilly checked off the last name.

"Nobody," she said, "nobody in our room could have taken Erin's locket."

Peanut's eyes danced. "That leaves only Miss Kraft. Do you suppose . . . ?"

They collapsed against each other, giggling. The idea of Miss Kraft taking anything that belonged to one of the kids was just too silly.

There was a tap on the door and Mrs. Butterman looked in. "May I come in?" she

asked. Without waiting for an answer, she went to the window seat, kicked off her shoes, and curled up on it. "There surely were a lot of lights on downstairs when I came in. I mean, considering that the two of you are holed up here."

"Forgot to turn 'em off," Peanut said airily.

"Think of using up energy that should not be wasted," said her mother. "Not to mention the light bill," she added.

"I hate it when you're not here when I come home," said Peanut. "The lights make the house cheerful."

"Sorry, dumpling," said Mrs. Butterman. "The dentist kept me waiting. And there were lines of people at the Jewel. I thought I'd never get to the check-out counter." Her eyes dropped to the list of names on the floor between Peanut and Jilly. "What are you up to?"

Peanut told her about the note in Erin's locker. "So I guess she's going to get her locket back," she finished. "At least it's not still hopelessly lost. Someone's found it."

"They've kept it for a long time," said Jilly.

"We're trying to figure out who wrote the note."

Mrs. Butterman was thoughtful. "You suspect one of your classmates?"

"Nobody seems like a person who wouldn't tell Erin the very instant they found it," said Peanut.

"I'm glad you decided that," said Mrs. Butterman. "I'm glad you know and trust your classmates."

Peanut and Jilly felt warm and good. They were glad, too, that they trusted the people in their room.

They headed for school the next morning with the locket problem still at the top of their list of things to think about. But it faded into the background when they saw Jennifer and her friends clustered in front of their lockers. They were watching Peanut and Jilly and talking behind their hands, snickering.

Peanut and Jilly passed them with their noses in the air, ignoring them — which was very hard to do.

"Listen," Peanut muttered as she pulled off

her jacket, "if you ever catch me snickering, poke me, will you? It's a really rotten habit."

Jilly considered this as she stuffed her jacket into her locker. "Maybe there are some things worth snickering about. Like, wouldn't you just love to snicker back at Jennifer?"

Peanut giggled. "Come on. Let's."

So they stared down the hall at Jennifer and Dawn and Cheryl, covered their mouths, and laughed behind their fingers.

"Do you think we're doing this right?" asked Peanut.

"They're looking daggers at us," said Jilly, "so I guess we are."

But somehow . . . somehow . . . snickering back at Jennifer and her pals wasn't satisfying. It didn't feel right.

"Oh, forget it," Peanut said after a minute.

"Who wants to be like them, anyway," said Jilly. "They're horrible kids."

They gathered together their books and went into class where another kind of trouble immediately caught everyone's attention.

Elvis went to the mouse house to check the food dish and water bottle.

"Wow!" he said. "We've got company."

"Company, Elvis?" Miss Kraft asked, going to look. "Oh," she said weakly. "Babies!"

"Six of them," said Elvis. "Look — they haven't got any hair yet. They're just pink skin. I wonder when their eyes will open."

"Elvis," said Miss Kraft, "we simply cannot keep eight mice in this room. You are going to have to figure out what to do about them."

"Okay," Elvis said cheerfully. "But can we just have fun watching them grow hair until I get a plan?"

Miss Kraft sighed.

"Listen! I've got an idea already." Elvis always had lots of ideas. He looked around at everybody. "Any of you guys want to adopt a mouse?" he asked.

There was silence.

"Only one to a customer," he added, "or there won't be enough to go around."

Nate snapped up the bait. "Neat," he said.

"I'll take one."

"Me, too," said Kevin. "Can we only have one apiece?"

"One," Elvis said firmly. "Just one."

"I want one," said Carrie.

"Me, too."

"I'll take one. I'll call mine Peaches."

"Peaches!"

"I can call it Peaches if I want to."

"Count me in!"

"Can I choose the one I want?"

"Maybe we can teach them to race with each other."

"Mine will beat yours."

"Who says so?"

"Hey!" Elvis looked around, counting on his fingers. "That's it. We're out of mice."

"Awwwwwww," sighed those who hadn't spoken up fast enough. "Awwwww."

"See?" Elvis said to Miss Kraft. "No problem."

CHAPTER
5

No problem is easier said than done. It takes cooperation from a lot of people. Namely parents.

Everyone was crowded around Elvis and the mouse house when Peanut and Jilly got to school the following morning. It took a minute to sort out what was going on.

"I can't," said Kevin. "My mother said she won't stay in the same house with a mouse."

"My folks said we had mice once, the regular kind," said Nate, "and I can't bring a mouse home. Not even a white one."

"No way — that's what my dad said," added Carrie.

"Nope." "I can't." "Me neither." Those were the words in the air, and Elvis was looking desperate.

"But look, guys, they're really neat pets."

Everyone drifted toward their desks. Elvis was left standing alone at Raidy and Yum's cage. For the first time ever, he looked dejected.

"If you don't take a chance on things, you're never going to have any fun," he said halfheartedly to the room in general.

"Parents have spoken, Elvis," said Miss Kraft. "Face the facts. You're going to have to find another answer to our mouse trouble."

Elvis dropped some corn and pieces of apple into the cage. "The babies will open their eyes pretty soon," he said. "And they're gonna have new baby mouse fur."

Everyone did feel sorry for him. An un-giggling Elvis was a very strange person, someone they hadn't met until that very moment.

They settled down to social studies and

everything was perfectly normal until recess. That's when Erin got another note. It was in her locker.

"Listen," she said excitedly, reading. " 'At eleven o'clock you will find something on the stairs. Come alone.' My locket," she breathed, looking around at the others. "I just know they're going to leave my locket on the stairs." She hugged herself, looking glad. "I'm going to get it back."

"But why on the stairs?" asked Peanut. "Why not just give it to you?"

"And why do you have to go alone?" asked Jilly.

"The alone part doesn't matter," said Erin. "You know how Miss Kraft is. She never lets us go to the bathroom in twos. She says we dawdle and don't come straight back to class."

"Can I see the note?" asked Peanut. "And have you got the other one?"

Erin gave both notes to her.

The first one was creased and wrinkled from having been read so much. Peanut and Jilly huddled together, comparing the notes.

"The printing looks the same."

"That's the same green marking pen — I'm sure of it."

"Who uses a green pen?"

"What a funny way of making a capital C."

"That Y is funny, too."

There weren't really any helpful clues in the notes.

"Well, let's hang onto them," said Jilly. "If more notes come, maybe we'll learn something."

That morning, as the minute hand on the wall clock jerked forward to the last minute of the ten o'clock hour, Erin raised her hand and asked to be excused. Miss Kraft gave permission and continued with the math lesson.

Three pairs of eyes watched Erin leave the room. Emmy looked hopeful. Jilly looked thoughtful. Peanut scowled because she didn't trust whoever had written the note.

Minutes later, Erin returned. The ribbon from her locket dangled limply from her fingers. She held it up and shook her head. No

locket. They had to wait until lunch to find out what had happened.

"It was tied around the railing," said Erin. "Look — it's muddy. It was a brand-new ribbon and now it's all dirty, like it was wet. And there was this note," she added, pulling a slip of paper from her pocket.

Like the others, it was printed in green marker ink:

This proves I've got the locket.
What will you trade for it?
Leave a note on page 327 of the big
dictionary in the Learning Center
at noon tomorrow.

They all gasped.

"That's ransom," sputtered Peanut. "Like somebody kidnapped your locket and now you've got to pay to rescue it."

Erin was downcast. "What else can I do? I've got to get it back. My aunt called us last night. She asked if I was enjoying the locket."

"What did you say?" asked Jilly.

"I said I love it a whole lot," said Erin. "And that's the truth. I didn't tell a lie." After a moment she added. "But I feel like I did."

"What are you going to trade?" asked Emmy.

"What would somebody want?" asked Erin.

"Nothing to wear. It might not fit," said Emmy.

"Oh," said Erin, remembering something. "My new funny-face earmuffs. I'll trade those. I hate to give them away." She looked forlorn. "But I'd rather have my locket."

Peanut and Jilly talked softly while Erin wrote her note.

"It just isn't fair," Peanut said hotly.

"Whoever is doing this is a really rotten kid," said Jilly.

Peanut became thoughtful. "You know, we can keep an eye on the LC and see who uses the dictionary."

"And who takes the note." Jilly became excited. "Let's rescue Erin's locket."

They looked at each other for a long moment.

"Let's catch whoever is doing this."

"Erin's going to get her locket back and keep her earmuffs, too."

They were going to see to it. They were going to make it happen.

CHAPTER
6

Erin left the note in the Learning Center right after lunch the next day.

"I hung around as long as I could," she reported when they settled down for class. "But I didn't see anybody come for the note."

Peanut and Jilly exchanged looks. They were going to get to the bottom of this.

"The note's still there," Peanut murmured to Jilly after her first excused absence from the room.

Jilly waited fifteen minutes and asked to be excused. She went straight to the Learning

Center, right to the big dictionary. She did her best to look busy, opening her notebook, writing a couple of words in it, before turning to page 327. Erin's note had not been touched.

Peanut made the next trip to the Learning Center twenty minutes later.

"My goodness!" said Mrs. Harris, coming up behind her. "The dictionary is certainly getting a workout today. You must be deep into a big project."

Peanut agreed that there was a project. She didn't say what kind, though — a rescue-Erin's-locket project.

She copied a word from page 325. She could feel a piece of paper under the page. Was it . . . ? Hastily she looked. It wasn't. It was just Erin's note, still there, waiting.

She smiled a polite thank you at Mrs. Harris as she left the Learning Center.

Mrs. Harris nodded. "I'm pleased you know how to use the unabridged dictionary."

Fifteen minutes passed. Jilly raised her hand.

Miss Kraft looked from Jilly to Peanut and

back again. "What's going on?" she asked.

Jilly didn't know what to say.

"I think there's been enough to-and-fro-ing for this afternoon," said Miss Kraft. "We'll stay in this room. Except for dire emergencies. And I *do* mean dire."

And so they didn't see who picked up the note from the dictionary.

Erin had an assigned time to go to the Learning Center almost an hour later. While Peanut and Jilly waited for her to come back, they worked on the A and W volumes of the encyclopedia. They were still looking up information on their chosen scientists.

Erin returned at last. "It was gone," she whispered, kneeling on the floor between them. "And there was another note there. Look at what this one says." She spread the note flat on the floor so they could see it.

Peanut and Jilly couldn't believe what they read. But there it was, written down, green on white. "Not good enough," read the note. "Autograph book would be okay, though."

Erin's voice quivered. "My autograph book is almost full. Last week I even got the autograph of my cousin's girlfriend because she actually has Michael Jackson's autograph. Someone's so mean," she said softly. "Really mean."

They watched as she scribbled a shaky "Okay" on the note.

Emmy came to find out what was going on. "I'll put it in the dictionary for you, Erin," she said kindly. "I haven't been to the lavatory yet. I think Miss Kraft will let me out of the room."

Miss Kraft did. And the reply to the note was in the dictionary when the four of them — Peanut and Jilly and Erin and Emmy — checked out the Learning Center before they went home.

They couldn't read it there, because Mrs. Harris seemed to be watching them even though she was stamping a date on a book for a little kid. They went outside and stood on the steps. Erin unfolded the note and they read it together.

Tomorrow morning at seven o'clock
put the autograph book in the hole
in the maple tree. Come alone.
Do not wait and watch.
Your locket will be there at recess.

"Do you suppose they mean it?" Erin asked at last. "Do you think they'll really give back my locket? Or will they keep the locket and the book, too?"

Who could say?

"You're taking a chance," said Emmy.

"I've got to," said Erin. "If I take the chance, I hope I'll get the locket back. If I don't take the chance, I surely won't."

She and Emmy headed for home together. Their shoulders slumped and they looked as though they were walking through sticky glue.

Peanut watched them go. "Erin's brave," she said. "She's willing to take a big chance."

Jilly was thoughtful. She didn't seem to hear Peanut. "Remember the story about the three pigs and the wolf?" she asked.

"What's that got to do — ?" Peanut started

to say, when she saw Jilly's face. "You're thinking of something, aren't you?"

"The smart pig," said Jilly. "Remember how he outsmarted the wolf?"

Every kid knows that story. "When the wolf told him to be somewhere at a certain time, the smart pig always went earlier," said Peanut.

"Uh-huh," said Jilly. "The wolf said to get to the turnip field at six o'clock, but — "

"But the smart pig got there at five o'clock," said Peanut. "Jillian Matthews, are you thinking what I think you're thinking?"

"We'd better be here at six o'clock tomorrow morning," Jilly said, grinning.

CHAPTER 7

Peanut was up and had Nibbsie out for his morning run and back in the house before her mother came downstairs to make breakfast. She left Nibbsie in the kitchen, noisily lapping at his water bowl as though he'd just spent a year in a desert.

Jilly was waiting for her at the corner. "I'm not supposed to leave for school so early," she said.

"My mom's going to have something to say when I get home this afternoon, I bet," said Peanut.

"Mine, too," said Jilly. "I left a note on the kitchen table."

Peanut wished she had thought to leave a note. And now that she was outdoors in the cool morning air, she wished she had thought to bring something to eat. She was starving. And she wouldn't get anything to eat until recess — and then only milk. It was going to be a long, hard morning.

The playground was empty so early in the day. Alcott School didn't look quite like itself in the golden morning light and without a lot of kids running around yelling and playing.

"Where's a good place to hide?" asked Peanut, looking around at the strange, deserted place.

"How about over there, on the steps leading down to the janitor's room?" said Jilly. "Nobody will see us and we can peek out between the railings."

They darted into the stairwell, hoping nobody was watching the playground.

The wait was a long one. Peanut's stomach kept growling, reminding her that she hadn't eaten breakfast, as they huddled on the cement steps, looking . . . watching. . . .

"There's Erin," Jilly said at last. "She's just coming around the corner. What time is it?"

"Two minutes to seven," said Peanut, checking her watch. "She sure does what she's told to do."

"It's got to be terrible, giving up her autograph book," said Jilly. "She told me she sleeps with it under her pillow sometimes."

"But she's going to get it back," Peanut reminded her. "And the locket, too."

They watched as Erin rolled to a stop on her bicycle and let it drop to the ground. She stood on tiptoe, looked into the hole in the tree, and slipped a plastic bag into the hole. Then — still following instructions exactly, not waiting around to see who came to get the book — she got back on her bike and whirled away toward home.

"If I were her, I'd sure come back and watch that tree," said Jilly.

"But if you really were Erin," said Peanut,

"you'd be desperate to get your locket back. So maybe you wouldn't hang around to watch."

"I wonder how long we'll have to wait now," said Jilly.

Peanut looked at her watch again. "It's only five past. Whoever's coming to get the book will surely come before lots of kids get here."

At exactly seven-thirty Peanut said, "I don't believe it! Well, yes, now that I think about it, I guess I do."

Jilly looked toward the street. "Jennifer Patimkin!" she gasped. "She's the one!"

"She's been watching Erin suffer all this time," Peanut muttered between clenched teeth, "and she didn't even care. Her heart must be made of stone."

"I'll bet she hasn't got a heart," said Jilly. "Maybe she's an alien from outer space and doesn't have earth-people feelings."

Jennifer spun into the schoolyard on her bicycle and slowed to a halt next to the maple tree. She glanced around in all directions, reached into the tree, and took out the plastic bag. She flipped through the autograph book,

smirking in self-satisfaction. At last she stuffed the book inside her jacket and pulled up the zipper. She took something from her pocket and dropped it into the hole in the tree and leaned down to pick up her bicycle.

"Now?" whispered Peanut.

"Now!" hissed Jilly.

Together they raced up the steps and headed for Jennifer, yelling.

"Okay, Jennifer Patimkin — the jig's up."

"We caught you red-handed."

Looking startled, Jennifer hopped onto her bicycle and, wobbling dangerously, headed toward the gate.

"She's going to get away," wailed Peanut.

"Run! We can catch her. Run!"

At that moment, Mr. Granger, Alcott School's principal, stepped out of the side door closely followed by Mrs. Harris. He blocked Jennifer's way and she skidded to a standstill.

"I'd like to talk to you, Jennifer," he said in his booming voice as Peanut and Jilly came near. "Will you show me what you have there inside your jacket?"

Mrs. Harris had gone to the tree. She came back holding out her hand, palm upward. "This locket was in the tree. I imagine it's the one Erin O'Malley lost."

"Is there something you'd like to tell me, Jennifer?" asked Mr. Granger.

Jennifer laughed nervously. "It's just a game we're playing," she said. "A silly game."

"It is not a game," Peanut contradicted her. "Not when you're the only one who knows the rules."

"It's not a game when Erin isn't having any fun," Jilly said heatedly.

"Let's go inside and talk about this," said Mr. Granger. "I want to hear more about this game." He looked at Peanut and Jilly. "Why don't you girls come along, too?"

He wasn't really asking — he was telling Peanut and Jilly to come. They followed him to his office.

He closed the door behind them.

"First," he said, "we'll begin with you, Polly and Jillian. What brought you to school so early this morning?"

Stepping on each others' words, they explained.

"Somebody had Erin's locket, only we didn't know who."

"We had to catch the person with the locket or taking Erin's autograph book."

"So we hid out and watched the tree this morning."

"We saw Erin bring her autograph book and put it in the hole in the tree. That's what the note told her she had to do."

"Then we saw Jennifer take the book and put something in the hole."

"But she almost got away."

They glared at Jennifer.

She looked down her nose at them. "Really," she said, "you are so childish. Playing detectives! I found Erin's locket on the floor beside the drinking fountain. Of course I was going to give it back to her. And of course I wasn't going to keep her dumb autograph book."

Mr. Granger leaned back in his chair. He stroked his chin thoughtfully. "All right, Polly. Okay, Jillian. You may go now. I'm glad you were looking after Erin's interests. But now Jennifer and I want to have a private little chat."

Peanut and Jilly turned to leave, glad to be getting out of Mr. Granger's office even though they weren't there for doing anything bad. They almost bumped into Mrs. Harris.

Peanut was the one with enough nerve to ask the question. She looked from Mrs. Harris to Mr. Granger. "How did you know about coming this morning? I mean, did somebody tell you?"

Mr. Granger and Mrs. Harris exchanged looks.

"Clairvoyance," said Mr. Granger. "We're both clairvoyant."

"You may look that word up in the dictionary," said Mrs. Harris.

And that's all they would say.

Peanut and Jilly stepped out into the hall.

"Grown-ups!" said Peanut. "I wish they'd give you a straight answer to a straight question."

"Know what I think?" said Jilly. "I think

Mrs. Harris read the notes in the dictionary."

"But it's not nice to read other people's mail," said Peanut. "That's what my mother said when I wanted to read Ceci's letter from Joe."

"None of this was nice," said Jilly. Then she brightened. "Well, yes, something *is* nice. Isn't Erin going to be happy!"

CHAPTER
8

■▼■▼■▼■▼■▼■▼■▼■▼■▼■▼■

"So I went to the Wild Garden Pet Shop after school yesterday," Elvis was saying.

Science class had begun. Everyone was there except Erin. Mrs. Perrin had come for Erin, saying that Mr. Granger wanted to see her.

"I told them about the mice," Elvis went on, "and they said they'd be glad to take them off my hands."

Waiting for Erin to come back, Peanut and Jilly were having trouble keeping their minds on their classwork — even something as interesting as Elvis's mice. How had Mr. Granger and Mrs. Harris found out about the tree and the autograph book and meeting at seven o'clock, before school began? And what was going to happen to Jennifer?

"That's a wonderful solution to your problem, Elvis," said Miss Kraft.

"Of course, they've got to see the mice first," said Elvis. "I mean, they want to be sure the mice are the white kind."

"Are they gonna pay you for them?" asked Ollie. "Are you gonna get rich out of this deal?"

Elvis shook his head. "They're gonna take them in trade."

"Listen, Dumbo," said Ollie. "Don't give them away for free."

"Oliver!" Miss Kraft said sharply. "Be still! Trade, Elvis? What kind of trade?"

"Well, see," said Elvis, "they've got this neat gerbil. He's worth more than the mice, so they said I can work off the difference. I'm gonna help clean the animals' cages. I guess I'll have to do that for a pretty long time before the gerbil is all mine."

"Check it out with your mother, Elvis," Miss Kraft advised. "Be sure she likes gerbils."

The door opened. Erin came in. She was clutching her autograph book to her chest, smiling blissfully. "I got it back," she said.

"And the locket?" asked Emmy. "What about the locket?"

"That, too." Erin held out her hand so that everyone could see the locket.

Peanut and Jilly smiled across the rows at each other. Erin had everything that belonged to her — including her nice great-aunt who she wasn't going to have to give up because of her lost-forever antique locket.

"Did Mrs. Harris say anything about the notes?" asked Jilly.

"When everybody kept going to the dictionary, she said she got very suspicious. She looked to see what we were doing and she saw the notes." Erin became thoughtful. "She said it's a terrible thing to use a great book like the dictionary for mischief. She said we abused it."

"Jennifer?" asked Peanut. "What's going to happen to her?"

"She's in a big pile of trouble," said Erin. "She had to apologize to me, and — "

"How neat!" Emmy exclaimed. "I'll bet that made you feel good!"

Erin bit her lip. "I felt funny," she said. Then she went on about Jennifer's troubles. "Her parents have to come to see Mr. Granger. And she's going to have to help Mrs. Harris in the library every day after school for a week. And she's got to write a report about games for Mr. Granger." Her forehead furrowed. "I wonder why she has to write about games."

Again Peanut and Jilly locked glances. *They* knew why Jennifer had to write about games.

Erin smiled, looking blissful once more. "I'm going to ask for a chain for my locket for Christmas. Then it'll never fall off again."

"Okay, people," said Miss Kraft. "We've had our full quota of distractions for the day. Let's get down to work. Polly? Jillian? Are you

ready to tell us what scientists you are? You said you work together."

They went to the front of the room.

"We did it," Peanut said happily. "We got Erin's book and locket back for her."

"We're a neat team," said Jilly.

Solemnly they shook hands. Then they turned to the class.

"Kitty," said Jilly.

"Hawk," said Peanut.

"Aw, you're easy. You're the Wright Brothers."

"You can't be men, lunkheads! You're girls."

"Who says we can't?"

"You aren't scientists! You're inventors."

"We found out things about air that nobody knew."

"Scientists and inventors — they explore things. They're the same, really."

"They are not!"

"Miss Kraft . . . Miss Kraft . . . are scientists and inventors the same or different?"

Things were back to normal in Miss Kraft's class at Louisa May Alcott School.